Contents

*Award-winner

Imagine

by Alison Lester

Imagine
if we were
crossing the icecap
where penguins toboggan
and arctic hares dash
where caribou snort
and killer whales crash...

beluga whale • narwhal • arctic dolphin • adele penguin

husky • arctic wolf • musk ox • arctic tern • snow goose • albatross • caribou • adel

puffin • elephant seal • emperor penguin • loon • lemming • sea lion • harp se

4

killer whale • humpback whale • narwhal • arctic dolphin •

enguin • snowy owl • arctic squirrel • walrus • harp seal • guillemot • kittiwake • herring •

guillemot • kittiwake • polar bear • narwhal • arctic hare • husky • loon •

Imagine
if we were
surrounded by monsters
where pteranodons swoop
and triceratops smash
where stegosaurs stomp
and tyrannosaurs gnash...

Imagine
if we were
away on safari
where crocodiles lurk
and antelope feed
where leopards attack
and zebras stampede...

gorilla • antelope • buffalo • elephant • cheetah • giraffe • jackal • baboon

chimpanzee • gazelle • ostrich • leopard • bushbaby • hippopotamus • wildebeest

12

ibex • impala • lion • crocodile • rhinoceros • colobus monkey • warthog

warthog • colobus monkey • rhinoceros • crocodile • lion • impala • ibex

hyena • mandrill • okapi • dik-dik • chimpanzee • gazelle • ostrich • leopard • bushbaby

That Was Some Daydream Mmmmmmm!

BY BERNARD WABER

I am going

to have a daydream.

I can feel it coming on.

But I don't want

to have a daydream.

I really don't want

to have a daydream.

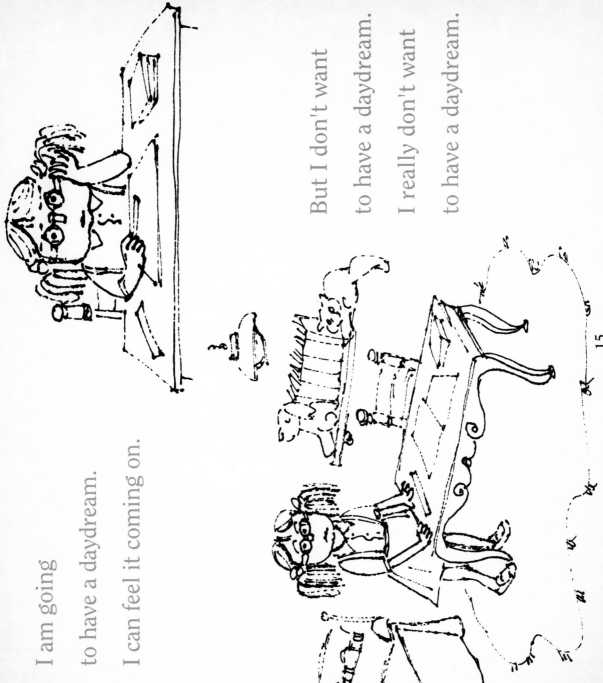

I am pinching myself
so I won't have
a daydream.

I am having
a glass of water
so I won't have
a daydream.

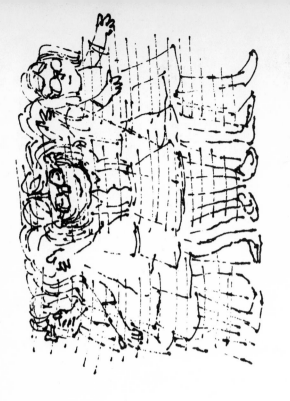

I am making

myself dizzy

so I won't have

a daydream.

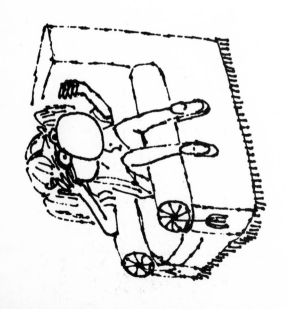

I am chewing

bubble gum

so I won't have

a daydream.

I am rolling

over and over

so I won't have

a daydream.

I don't want
to have a daydream.
I really don't want
to have a daydream.

I will think about arithmetic...
and how if I have a dozen pears
and I give away seven
I would then have...

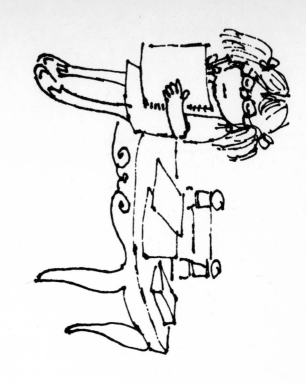

I would then have...

a daydream.

On the Merry-Go-Round

by bp Nichol

On the Merry-Go-Round
the horse makes no sound,
but she takes me so far
and she takes me so high
I can ride to the edge of the sky.

22

On the Merry-Go-Round
the dog makes no sound,
but he runs on so swift
as I cling to his back
I can ride to the moon and ride back.

23

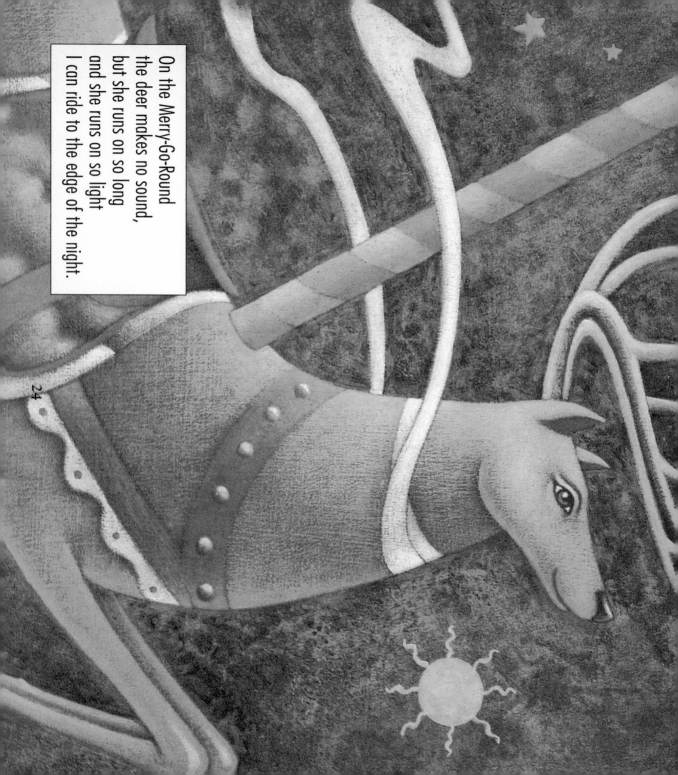

On the Merry-Go-Round
the deer makes no sound,
but she runs on so long
and she runs on so light
I can ride to the edge of the night.

24

On the Merry-Go-Round
if I make no sound
I'm the dog in his race
and the deer in her leap
and the horse that I'll ride into sleep,
and the horse that I'll ride into sleep.

25

No Dinosaurs in the Park

BY DOROTHY JOAN HARRIS

When Grandpa comes to visit
we always go to the park.
We walk along the path, past the pond and
the rock garden, and look at everything.
Sometimes I play on the swings
while Grandpa pushes me.
Sometimes we sit on a bench
and Grandpa tells me stories.
I almost always ask for stories
about dinosaurs.

Today, while we were walking by the pond,
Grandpa stopped all of a sudden and said,
"Bless my socks! Just look over there –
a diplodocus!"
I looked where he was pointing,
but all I could see was a big branch
floating on the pond.

"Do you see its long, long tail sticking out
of the water?" asked Grandpa.
"That tail can flick like a whip, you know."
Well, then I saw it.
"We'd better hide!" I shouted.
The huge diplodocus flicked its tail,
but we hid behind a tree.
"He won't be able to reach us here,"
Grandpa said.

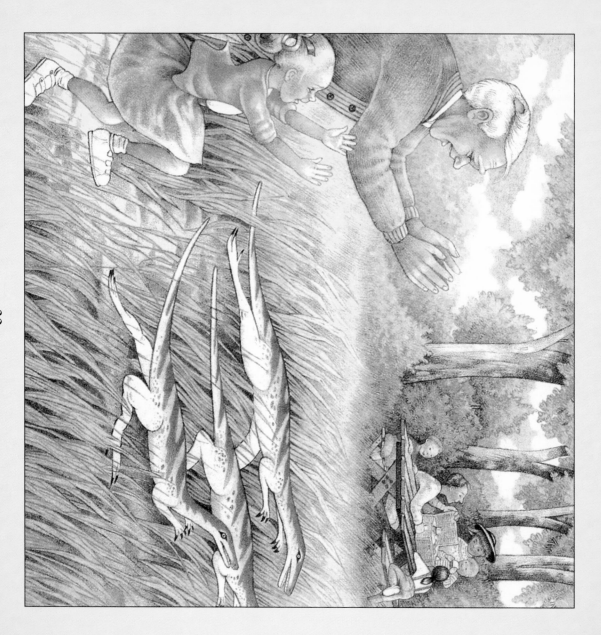

Just after we escaped from the diplodocus,
Grandpa stopped again. "Shhh!" he whispered.
"Look over there – a compsognathus.
A whole gang of them, in fact."

I looked toward the tall grass. At first
I thought it was a bunch of noisy crows.
"A compsognathus is small," Grandpa said,
"but it's speedy. I think this gang is hunting
for their dinner."

"They look hungry," I agreed.
"Do you think they'll try to eat us?"
"Probably not," said Grandpa, "but maybe
we should scare them away, just in case."
So we roared and we shouted,
and they all ran away.
"A compsognathus doesn't like loud noises,"
said Grandpa.

31

Suddenly a great winged shape flew overhead.
"Look out! A pterodactyl!" shouted Grandpa.
"Red alert! Red alert!"
The other people in the park probably thought
it was a Canada goose. But we could see
what it really was.

We stood very still until it was gone.
"Pterodactyls can't see you
if you stand very still," I told Grandpa.

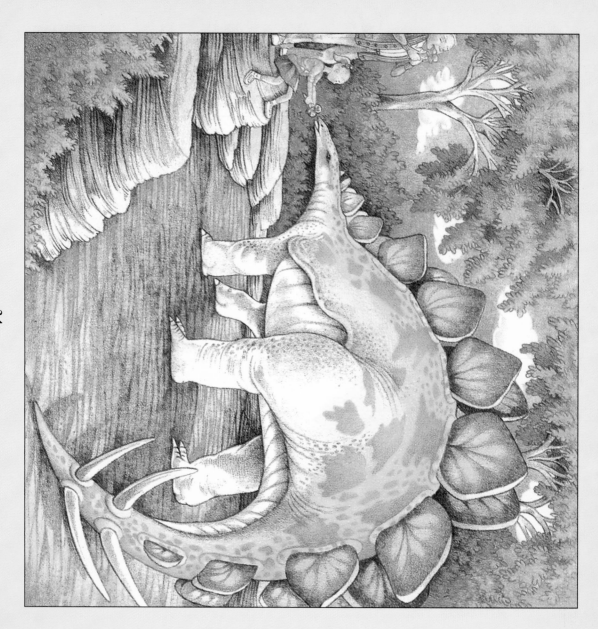

On the way home we walked past
the rock garden.
All of a sudden *I* stopped. "Look, Grandpa!"
I said. "There's a stegosaurus in those rocks!"
"Well, I'll be hornswoggled," said Grandpa,
"so there is! He must be trying to hide.
A stegosaurus is a very timid creature,
you know."

We coaxed him out with a chocolate
ice cream cone. He really liked it,
but he was a messy eater and splashed
all over my new shirt.

When we got home, I told Mom
why my shirt was such a mess.
She was a bit cross about it.
And she said there are absolutely
no dinosaurs in the park.
But Grandpa and I know better.

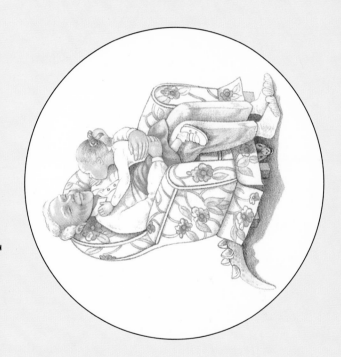

37

Fact or Fantasy?

Nothing is bigger than a dinosaur.

The giant Ultrasaurus may be
the largest land animal that ever lived.
It was 100 feet long and weighed
about 85 tons. But . . .
there is an animal alive today
that is even bigger — the blue whale.

Blue whales are over 100 feet long
and they weigh more than 160 tons.

38

Fact or Fantasy?

All snakes are slimy.

Some people think snakes are slimy, but this isn't so. When a snake is out of water, its skin is dry and cool.

A snake's body is covered with hard scales that overlap. These scales protect the snake from harm.

Fact or Fantasy?

Octopuses squeeze their victims.

Stories about octopuses squeezing their prey are not true. Many octopuses are only a few inches across. But even the biggest octopuses rarely hurt people. Octopuses are usually shy and they hide between rocks under water.

An octopus never strangles or crushes its prey. It does use its tentacles, though, to hold an animal still until it can bite it with its beak.

Fact or Fantasy?

Mount Everest is taller than all other mountains.

Surprise! Mount Everest is not taller than all other mountains.

The tallest mountains in the world were difficult to find because they are under water. Mauna Kea in the Hawaiian Islands is one of these underwater mountains. It is the world's tallest mountain.

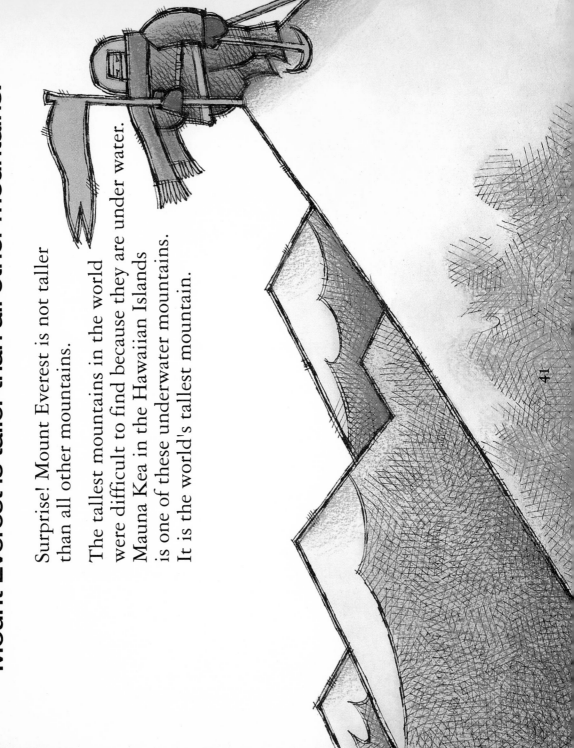

Fact or Fantasy?

The moon is made of cheese.

Some people think that the moon looks like it's made of green cheese. But of course it isn't.

Years ago astronauts traveled to the moon. They brought back samples of the moon's surface. Scientists studied this material and discovered that the moon is really made of rock. We have the same type of rock on Earth.

Architect
of the Moon

by Tim Wynne-Jones

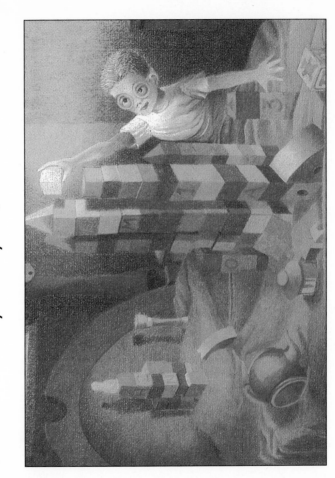

A message arrived from outer space, a message from the Moon.

Help! I'm falling apart. Yours, the Moon.

Luckily it arrived at the home
of brave block-builder David Finebloom.
David waved from his window.
"Don't worry, Moon."

He gathered all the things he would need for a busy night's work and told his mom not to wait up.

Back in his room he laid out a launch pad and turned the dial to Moon.
He activated his spaceship and Whooosh!
He was off.

45

He arrived just in time and started right in.
First the floor of the tranquil sea,
then the valleys, hills and mountains.
He had brought all the right shapes and
all the right colors.

Bigger, bigger, bigger grew the Moon,
and rounder, too. Course upon course,
layer upon layer, until it was done;
it was full. Hurray for David Finebloom!

It was a little rough in places,
but who on Earth would notice.

47

David waved from his spaceship. "Don't worry, Mom!" He set the dial for home and got there just in time for breakfast on the porch. A perfect five-minute egg.